OLD HOGGEN

A MYSTERY

OLD HOGGEN

A MYSTERY

BRAM STOKER

WILDSIDE PRESS

The text for this edition is taken from the May 13, 1893 appearance in *The Courier-Journal* (a newspaper) of Louisville, Kentucky.

Published by Wildside Press LLC.
www.wildsidebooks.com

OLD HOGGEN: A MYSTERY (1893)

"If he had the spirit of a man in him, he would go himself," said my mother-in-law.

"Indeed, I think you might, Augustus. I know I often deny myself and make efforts to please you, and you know that my dear mamma loves crabs," said my mother-in-law's daughter.

"Far be it from me to interfere," said Cousin Jemima, as they call her, smoothing down her capstrings as she spoke. "But I do think that it would be well if Cousin Kate—who, like myself, is not at all so strong as she looks—could have something to tempt her appetite."

Cousin Jemima, who was my mother-in-law's cousin, was as robust as a Swiss guide, and had the appetite and digestion of a wild Indian. I began to get riled.

"What on Earth are you all talking about?" said I. "One would think you were all suffering some terrible wrong. You want crabs—and you are actually now engaged in bolting down one of the biggest crabs I ever saw. What does it all mean? Unless, indeed, you want merely to annoy me!"

Here my mother-in-law laid down her fork in a majestic way and glared at me, saying:

"If there are no crabs nearer than Bridport, then you must go there," while her daughter began to cry.

This, of course, settled the matter. When my mother-in-law has a go in at me I can—although it makes me uncomfortable and unhappy—stand it; but when her daughter cries, I am done: so I made an effort by an attempt at jocularity—feeble, though, it was—to grace my capitulation and go out with the honors of war.

"I shall get you some crabs," said I, "my dear mother-in-law, which even you will not be able to vanquish—or even, Cousin Jemima, with her feeble digestion."

They all looked very glum, so I made another effort.

"Yes," I went on. "I shall bring you some giant crabs, even if I have to find Old Hoggen first."

The only answer made in words was by my mother-in-law, who cut in sharply: "If Old Hoggen was as great a brute as you, I don't wonder that he has got rid of—"

Cousin Jemima endorsed the sentiment with a series of sniffs and silences, as eloquent and expressive as the stars and negative chapters of Tristram Shandy. Lucy looked at me, but it was a good look, more like my wife's, and less like that of my mother-in-law's daughter than had hitherto been, so tacitly we became a linked battalion.

There was a period of silence, which was broken by my mother-in-law:

"I do not see—I fail to see why you will always introduce that repulsive subject."

As she began the battle, and as Lucy was now on my side, I did not shun the fight, but made a counter attack.

"Crabs?" I asked interrogatively, in a tone which I felt to be dangerous.

"No, not crabs—how dare you call the subject of my food—and you know how delicate an appetite I have—disgusting—"

"Well, what do you mean?" I inquired, again showing the green lamps.

"I call 'disgusting' the subject of conversation on which you always harp—that disreputable old man whom they say was murdered. I have made inquiries—many inquiries—concerning him, and I find that his life was most disreputable. Some of the details of his low amours which I have managed to find out are most improper. What do you think, Cousin Jemima—"

Here she whispered to the other old dear, who eagerly inclined her ear to listen.

"No, really! Seventeen? What a wretched old man," and Cousin Jemima became absorbed in a moral reverie.

My mother-in-law went on:

"When you, Augustus, bring perpetually before our notice the name of this wicked man, you affront your wife."

Here the worm, which had hitherto been squirming about trying to imagine that it was built on the lines of a serpent, which can threaten and strike, turned, and I spoke.

"I do not think it is half so bad to mention a topic of common interest, and which is forced upon us every hour of every day since we came here, as it is for you to make such a charge. I respect and love my wife too much"—here I pulled Lucy toward me, who came willingly—"to affront her even by accident. And, moreover, I think, madam, that it would be better if, instead of making such preposterous and monstrous charges, you would give me a little peace at my meals by holding your tongue and giving yourself an opportunity of getting tired and sick of crabs. I have not sat down to a meal since I came here that you have not spoiled it with your quarrelling. You quite upset my digestion. Can't you let me alone?"

The effect of the attack was appalling.

My mother-in-law, who had by this time finished the last morsel of the crab, sat for a moment staring and speechless, and for the only time in her life burst into tears.

Her tears were not nearly so effective upon me as Lucy's, and I sat unmoved. Cousin Jemima, with an inborn tendency to rest secure on the domineering side, said, audibly:

"Served you quite right, Cousin Kate, for interrupting the man at his supper."

Lucy said nothing, but looked at me sympathetically.

Presently my mother-in-law, with a great effort, pulled herself together and said:

"Well, Augustus, perhaps you are right. We have suffered enough about Old Hoggen to make his name familiar to us."

* * * *

Indeed we suffered. The whole history of Old Hoggen had for some weeks past been written on our souls in the darkest shade of ink. We had come to Charmouth hoping to find in that fair spot the peace that we yearned for after the turmoil and troubles of the year. With the place we were more than satisfied, for it is a favored spot. In quiet, lazy Dorsetshire it lies, close to the sea, but sheltered from its blasts. The long straggling village of substantial houses runs steeply down the hillside parallel to the seaboard. Everywhere are rivulets of sweet water, everywhere are comfort and seeming plenty. A smiling and industrious peasantry are the normal inhabitants, among whom the good old customs of salutation have not died away. A town-made coat enacts a bob courtesy from the females and a salute in military fashion from the men, for the young men are all militia or volunteers.

We had been at Charmouth some three weeks. Our arrival had caused us to swell with importance, for, from the time we left Axminster in the diurnal omnibus till our being deposited at our pretty cottage, bowered in enticing greenery and rich with old world flowers, our advent seemed to excite interest and attention. Naturally I surmised that the rustic mind was overcome by the evidence of metropolitan high tone manifested in our clothes and air. Lucy put it down—in her own mind which her mother kindly interpreted for her—to the striking all-the-world-over effect of surpassing loveliness. Cousin Jemima attributed it to their respect for blood; and my mother-in-law took it as a just homage to the rare, if not unique, union of birth, grace, gentleness, breeding, talent, wisdom, culture and power—as embodied in herself. We soon found, however, that there was a cause different from all these.

There had lately come to light certain circumstances tending to show that we were objects of suspicion rather than veneration.

Some days before our arrival great excitement had been caused in Charmouth by the disappearance, and, consequently, rumored murder, of an old inhabitant, one Jabez Hoggen, reputed locally to be of vast wealth and miserly in the extreme. This good reputation brought him much esteem, not just in Charmouth alone, but through the country round, from Lyme Regis on the one hand as far as distant Bridport on the other.

Even inland the trumpet note of Old Hoggen's wealth sounded to Axminster and even to Chard. This good repute of wealth was, however, the only good repute he had, for his social misdoings were so manifold and continuous as to interest all the social stars of Lyme. These are old ladies who inhabit the snug villas in the uplands at Lyme, and who claim as their special right the covered seats on the Madeira walk of that pretty town, and who are so select that they will not even associate with others except in massed groups or nebulae. Old Hoggen's peccadilloes afforded them a fertile theme for gossip. There was an inexhaustible store of minute and wicked details of this famous sinner.

Year after year Old Hoggen moved among the law-abiding inhabitants of Charmouth, wallowing in his wickedness and adding to his store of goods in the here and ills in the hereafter.

Strange to say, all this time not once—not even once—did the Earth yawn and swallow him. On the contrary, he flourished. No matter what weather came he always benefited. Even if the raid did destroy one of his crops, it made another flourish exceedingly. When there was a storm, he accumulated sea rack; when there was calm, he got fish. Many of his neighbors began to have serious doubts about the Earth ever yawning and swallowing at all; and even the old ladies in Lyme Regis—those who had passed the age of proposals and begun to regret, or at least to reconsider, their youth—sometimes thought that perhaps immortality was a little too harshly condemned after all.

Suddenly this old man disappeared, and Charmouth woke up to the fact that he was the best known, the most respected, the most important person in the place. His ill-doing sank into insignificance, and his good stood revealed in gigantic proportions. Men pointed out his public spirit, the reforms he had instituted, the powers he had developed; women called attention to the tenderness he had always exhibited to their sex, unworthy as had been the examples of the same that had darkened the horizon of his life. More than one wise matron was heard to remark that if his lot in life had been to meet one good woman, instead of those hussies, his manner of life might have been different.

It is a fact worth notice that in the logic of might-have-been, which is pitying woman's pathway to heaven, the major premise is pitying woman.

However, were his life good or ill, Old Hoggen had disappeared, and murder was naturally suspected. Two suppositions—no one knew whence originating—were current. The most popular was that some of his unhappy companions, knowing of his wealth and greedy of his big gold watch and his diamond ring, had incited to his murder other still more disreputable companions. The alternative belief was that some of his relations—for he was believed to have some, although no one had ever seen or heard of them—had quietly removed him so that in due time they might in legal course become possessed of his heritage.

Consequent upon the latter supposition suspicion attached itself to every newcomer. It was but natural that the vulture-like relatives should appear upon the scene as soon as possible, and eager eyes scanned each fresh arrival. As I soon discovered, my respected connection by marriage, Cousin Jemima, bore a strong resemblance to the missing man, and drew around our pretty resting place the whole curiosity of Charmouth and concentrated there the attention of the secret myrmidons of the law.

In fact, the Charmouth policeman haunted the place, and strange men in slop clothes and regulation boots came from Bridport and Lyme Regis, and even from Axminster itself.

These latter representatives of the intellectual subtlety of Devon, Dorset, and Wilts were indeed men full of wile and cunning of device. The bucolic mind in moments of unbending, when frank admission of incompleteness is a tribute to good fellowship, may sometimes admit that its working are slow, but even in the last stage of utter and conscious drunkenness one quality is insisted on—surety.

Of surety, in simple minds the correlation is tenacity of purpose and belief.

Thus it was that when once the idea of our guilt had been mooted and received, no amount of evidence, direct or circumstantial, could obliterate the idea from the minds of the rustic detectives. These astute men, one by one, each jealous of the other, and carrying on even among themselves the fiction of non-identification, began to seek the evidences of our guilt. It struck me as a curious trait in the inhabitants of the diocese of Salisbury that their primary intellectual effort had one tendency, and that all their other efforts were subordinate to this principle. It may have been that the idea arose from historical contemplation of the beauty of their cathedral and an unconscious effort to emulate the powers of its originators.

Or it may not have been.

But, at all events, their efforts took the shape of measuring. I fail myself to see how their measurements, be they never so accurate, could in anywise have helped them. Further, I can not comprehend how the most rigid and exact scrutiny in this respect could have even suggested a combination of facts whence a spontaneous idea could have emanated. Still, they measured, never ceasing day or night for more than a week, and always surreptitiously. They measured one night the whole of the outside of our cottage. I heard them in the night, out on the roof, crawling about like gigantic cats, and, although we learned that one man had fallen off the roof and broken his arm, we were never officially informed of the fact. They made incursions into the house, under various pretexts, there to endeavor to measure the interior.

In every case a ruse was adopted. One morning, while we were out bathing, a man called to measure the gas pipes, and, after going through several of the rooms taking the dimensions of the walls, was informed by the servant that there was no gas, not only in the house, but in the village. Not being prepared with a further excuse, he said, with that nonchalance he could assume, that "it was no matter," and went away. Another time a British workman, as he styled himself, arrayed in cricket flannels and a straw hat, came to look at the kitchen boiler for the landlord, and asked that he might begin on the roof. I saw the inevitable rule and tape measure, and told him that the landlord's house was next door, and that he would find the boiler buried in the garden. He withdrew, thanking me with effusion, and making a note of the words "buried in the garden" in his notebook.

Another day a man called with fish—he had only one sole and that he carried in his hand. The cook was out and I told him we would have it. He asked if he might go into the garden to skin it. I told him he might, and went out. When I came back in about an hour's time, I found him there still, measuring away. He had got all the dimensions of the garden and the walls, and was now engaged on the heights of the various flowers. I asked him what the dickens he was doing there still, and why he was measuring. He answered vaguely that he was not measuring.

"Why, man alive," said I, "don't tell me such a story—I saw you at it—why, you are doing it still," as indeed he was.

He stood up and answered me:

"Well, sir, I will tell you why. I was looking to see if I could find room to bury the skin of the sole."

He had not skinned the sole, which lay on a flag in the hot sunshine, and was beginning to look glassy.

They even measured as well as they could the height of the members of the family. When any of us passed a wall where any of these men were, he immediately spotted some place on the wall of equal height, and the moment we passed, out came the rule and he measured it.

Our cook was asked one night by a tall man to lay her head on his shoulder. She did so, as she told us afterward being so surprised that she did not know what to do. When she came in we saw on her black bonnet a series of reversed numbers in chalk dying away over the temple with 5 ft. 6-1/2 in.

Cousin Jemima, who was of a full habit of body—to say the least of it—was one evening stopped in the lane by two men, who put their arms round her waist from opposite sides. She distinctively said that they had something that looked like a long rope marked in yards, or, as she persisted, in chains, which, when she had escaped from them, they examined with seeming anxiety, and made some entry in books which they carried, laughing all the time heartily and digging each other in the ribs as they pointed at her.

Our dog was often measured, and one afternoon there was a terrible caterwauling, which we found to arise from a respectable man trying to weigh our cat in an ouncel, borrowed from a neighboring shop.

My mother-in-law, who had no suspicion whatever that she was an object of suspicion, waxed at times furiously indignant at the rudeness of the loiterers round our door, and now and again comported herself so violently as to cause them serious fright. I was unaware during the time of my courtship that this remarkable woman possessed such a power of invective. She certainly proved herself a consummate actress in concealing it as she did; for during that time of rapture and agony I enjoyed the contemplation and experienced the practical outcome of a sympathy and sweetness as ripe as unalloyed. My wife and I both understood the motives of the local detectives, and always recognized them under their disguises. It was a never-ending source of mirth to us to enjoy the spectacle of Cousin Jemima's ungratified curiosity, and of my mother-in-law's periodic anger. For the purposes of our own amusement we filled up the daily blanks caused by the slackness of the executive in keeping perpetually before them the theme of Old Hoggen. I amused myself by keeping a little note book, in which I jotted down all kinds of odd measurements for the purpose of leaving it about sometime to puzzle the detectives.

Thus it came about that the repulsive individuality of Old Hoggen became, in a manner, of interest to us, and his name to be interwoven in the web of our daily converse.

I knew that to mention Old Hoggen to my mother-in-law, when previously influenced by hunger or any collateral vexation, would have the effect of a red rag on a bull, and, as has been seen, I was not disappointed.

Now, however, that supper was over and the crab had been all consumed, I found myself pledged to discover by the morrow a full supply of that succulent food. I did not let the matter distress me, as I anticipated a delightful walk by the shore to Bridport, a walk which I had not yet undertaken. In the morning I awoke early, just a little after daybreak, and, leaving my wife asleep, started on my walk.

The atmosphere of the early dawn was delightful and refreshing, and the sight of the moving sea filled me with a great pleasure, notwithstanding the fact that an ominous shower on the water and a cold wind foretold a coming storm.

At this part of the Dorset coast the sea makes perpetual inroads on the land. As all the country is undulating, the shore presents from the sea an endless succession of steep cliffs, some of which rise by comparison to a scale of moderate grandeur.

The cliffs are either of blue clay or sandstone, which soft or friable material perpetually gives way under the undermining influence of the tides assisted by the exfiltration of springs, causing an endless series of moraines. The beach is either of fine gravel or of shingle, save at places where banks of half-formed rock full of fossils run into the sea.

The shingle, which forms the major portion of the road, makes walking at times trying work.

I passed by the target for a rifle practice, and the spot reserved tacitly as the bathing place for gentlemen, and so on under the first headland, the summits of whose bare yellow cliff is fringed with dark pine trees bent eastwards by the prevailing westerly breeze.

Here the shingle began to get heavier. It had been driven by successive tides and storms into a mass like a snow drift, and it was necessary to walk along the top of the ridge whence the pebbles rolled down every step.

The wind had now begun to rise, and as I went onward the waves increased in force till the whole shore was strewn with foam swept from the crests of the waves. Sometimes great beds of seaweed—a rare commodity on the Dorset coast—rose and fell as the waves rolled in and broke.

On I went as sturdily as I could. The blue-black earth of the Charmouth cliffs had now given place to sandstone, and great boulders shaped like mammoth bones—as indeed they probably were—cumbered the foreshore. I stopped to examine some of these, ostensibly from scientific interest, but in reality to rest myself. I was now getting a little tired, and more than a little hungry, for when starting I had determined to eat my breakfast at Bridport, and to test the culinary capabilities of the place.

As I sat on the stones looking seaward, I noticed something washing in and out among the boulders. On examination it proved to be a hat—a human hat. I hooked it in with a piece of driftwood. I turned it over, and in turning it saw something white stuck within the leather lining. Gingerly enough I made an examination, and found the white mass to be some papers, on the outside of one of which was the name "J. Hoggen."

"Hullo!" said I to myself. "Here is some news of Old Hoggen at last." I took the papers out, carefully squeezed the wet out of them, as well as I could between flat stones, and put them in the pocket of my shooting jacket. I placed the hat on a boulder and looked round to see if I could find any further signs of the missing man. All the while the breeze was freshening and the waves came rolling in in increasing volume.

Again I saw, some twenty yards out, something black floating, bobbing up and down with each wave. After a while I made it out to be the body of a man. By this time my excitement had grown to intensity, and I could hardly await the incoming of the body borne by the waves.

On and on it came, advancing a little with each wave, till at last it got so close that reaching out I hooked part of the clothing with my piece of timber, and pulled the mass close to the shore.

Then I took hold of the collar of the coat and pulled. The cloth, rotten with the sea water, tore away, and left the piece in my hand.

With much effort—for I had to be very careful—I brought the body up on the beach, and began to make an accurate examination of it.

While doing so I found in the pocket a tape measure, and it occurred to me that I must fulfill all the requirements of the local police, and so began to take dimensions of the corpse.

I measured the height, the length of the limbs, of the hands and feet. I took the girth of the shoulders and the waist, and, in fact, noted in my pocketbook a sufficiency of detail to justify a tailor in commencing sartorial operations on a full scale. Some of the dimensions struck me at the time as rather strange, but having verified the measurements I noted them down.

On examination of the clothes and pockets, I found the massive gold watch hanging on the chain and the big diamond ring, to whose power of inspiring greed local opinion had attributed the murder. These I put in my pocket together with the purse, studs, papers and money of the dead man. In making the examination the coat became torn, revealing a mass of bank notes between cloth and lining: in fact, the whole garment was quilted with them. There was also a small note case containing the necessary papers for a voyage to Queensland by a ship leaving Southampton the previous week.

These discoveries I thought so valuable that I felt it my duty to try to bring the body to the nearest place of authority, which I considered would probably be Chidiock, a village on the Bridport road which I had seen upon the map.

It was now blowing a whole gale, and the waves broke on the beach in thunder, dragging down the shingle in their ebb with a loud screaming. The rain fell in torrents, and the increasing of the storm decided me in my intention to carry the body with me.

I lifted it across my shoulder with some difficulty, for at each effort the cloths, already torn in the extrication of paper money, fell to pieces. However, at last I got it on my shoulder, face downwards, and started. I had hardly taken a step when, with an impulse which I could not restrain, I let it slip—or, rather, threw it—to the ground.

It had seemed to me to be alive. I certainly felt a movement. As it lay all in a heap on the beach, with the drenching rain sweeping the pale face, I grew ashamed of my impulse, and, with another, effort, took it up and started again.

Again there was the same impulse, with the same cause—the body seemed alive. This time, however, I was prepared, and held on, and after a while the idea wore away.

Presently I came to a place where a mass of great boulders strewed the shore. The stepping from one to another shook me and my burden, and as I jumped from the last of the rocks to the smooth sand which lay beyond I felt a sudden diminution of weight. As my load overbalanced, I fell on the sand higgledy piggledy with my burden.

Old Hoggen had parted in the middle.

As may be imagined, I was not long getting up. On a survey of the wreck I saw, to my intense astonishment, some large crabs walking out of the body. This, then, explained the strange movement of the corpse. It occurred to me that the presence of these fishes was incontrovertible proof that crabs did exist between Bridport and Lyme Regis, and not without a thought of Cousin Jemima and my mother-in-law, I lifted two or three and put them in the big pocket of my shooting coat.

Then I began to consider whether I should leave the departed Hoggen where he was or bring him on.

For a while I weighed the arguments pro and con, and finally concluded to bring him on with me, or it, or them, or whatever the fragments could be called. It was not an alluring task, in any aspect, and it was by a great effort that I undertook the duty.

I gathered the things together, and a strange looking heap they made—waxen limbs protruding from a wet heap of dishevelled rags. Then I began to lift them. It had been a task of comparative ease carrying the body over my shoulder, but now I had to pick up separate pieces and carry them altogether in my hands and under my arms. Often I had laughed, as I went through Victoria street, to see people of both sexes, worthy, but deficient of organizing power and system, coming forth from the co-operative stores bearing hosts of packages purchased without system in the various departments. Such a one I now felt myself to be. Do what I would, I could not hold all at one time the various segments of my companion. Just as I had carefully tucked the moieties of Old Hoggen under my arms, I spied some of his clothing on the shore, and in trying to raise these also lost a portion of my load. What added to the aggravation of the situation was that the wear and tear began to tell upon the person of the defunct. Thus while I was lifting the upper section, an arm came away, and from the lower a foot.

However, with a supreme effort I bundled the pieces together, and, lifting the mass in my arms, proceeded on my way. But now the storm was raging in full force, and I saw that I must hurry or the advancing waves, every moment rushing closer to the cliffs, would cut me off. I could see, through the blinding rain, a headland before me, and knew that if I could once pass it I would be in comparative safety.

So I hurried on as fast as I could, sometimes losing a portion of my burden, but never being able to wait to pick it up. Had my thoughts and ejaculations been recorded they would have been somewhat as follows:

"There goes a hand; it was lucky I took off the ring."

"Half the coat; well that I found the bank notes."

"There goes the waistcoat; a fortunate thing I have the watch."

"A leg off—my! Will I ever get him home?"

"Another leg."

"An arm gone."

"His grave will be a mile long."

"We must consecrate the shore that he may lay in hallowed ground."

"The lower trunk gone, too. Poor fellow; no one can hit him now below the belt."

"An arm gone, too; he would not be able to defend himself if they did."

"Murder! But he's going fast."

"The clothes all gone, too—I had better have left him where he was."

"Ugh! There goes the trunk; nothing left now but the head."

"Ugh! That was a close shave anyhow. Never mind, I will keep you safe."

I clung tight to the head, which was now my sole possession of the corpse.

It was mighty hard to hold it, for it was as slippery as glass, and the tight holding of it cramped my efforts and limited me as I leaped from rock to rock or dashed through the waves, which now touched in their onward rush to the base of the cliff.

At least, through the blinding rain, I saw the headland open, and with a great rush through the recoil of a big wave I rounded it and rested for a moment to breathe on the wide shore beyond.

Then I tried for a while to collect my scattered faculties, such being the only part of the goods scattered in the last half-hour which could be collected.

I felt ruefully that my effort to bring to the rites of burial the body of Old Hoggen had been a mistaken one. All had gone save the head which lay on the sand, and whose eyes actually seemed to wink at me as the flukes of the spume settled over the eyes, dissolving as the bubbles burst. The property was, I felt, safe enough. I put my hand into the pocket of my shooting coat but in an instant drew it out again with a scream of pain, for it had been severely nipped. I had forgotten the crabs.

Very carefully I took out one of these fish and held him legs upward, he making frantic efforts to seize me with his claws. He seemed a greedy one, indeed, for he was trying to eat the diamond ring which he had got half within that mysterious mouth which is covered with a flap like that over the lock of a portmanteau. Hence also projected part of the watch chain. I found that the brute had actually swallowed the watch, and it was with some difficulty that I relieved from his keeping both it and the ring. I took care to place the valuable property in the other pocket where the crabs were not.

Then I took up my head—or, rather Old Hoggen's—and started on my way, carrying the final relic under my arm.

The storm began to decrease, and died away as quickly as it had arisen, so that, before I had traversed half the long stretch of sand that lay before me, instead of storm there was marked calm, and for blinding rain an almost insupportable heat.

I struggled on over the sand, and at length saw an opening in the cliff—which, on coming close, I found to be caused by a small stream which had worn a deep cleft in the blue-black earthy rock, and, falling and tumbling from above, became lost in the beach.

There was a look about the sand here that seemed to me to me somewhat peculiar. Its surface was smooth and shining, with a sort of odd dimple here and there. It looked so flat and inviting after my scramble over the rock and shingle and plodding through the deep sand, that with joy I hurried toward it—and at once began to sink.

By the odd shiver that traversed it I knew that I was being engulfed in quicksand.

It was a terrible position.

I had already sunk over my knees and knew that unless aid came I was utterly lost. I would at that moment have welcomed even Cousin Jemima.

It is the misfortune of such people as her that they never do make an appearance at a favorable time—such as this.

But there was no help—on one side lay the sea with never a sail in sight, and the waves still angry from the recent storm tumbling in sullenly upon the shore—on the other side was a wilderness of dark cliff; and along the shore on either way an endless waste of sand.

I tried to shout, but the misery and terror of the situation so overcame me that my voice clung to my jaws, and I could make no sound. I still kept Old Hoggen's head under my arm. In moments of such danger the mind is quick to grasp an offered chance, and it suddenly occurred to me that, if I could get a foothold even for a moment, I might still manage to extricate myself. I was as yet but on the edge of the quicksand, and but a little help would suffice. With the thought came also the means—Old Hoggen's head.

No sooner thought than done.

I laid the head on the sand before me, and pressing on it with my hands, felt that I was relieving my feet of part of their weight. With an effort I lifted one leg and placed the foot on the head now embedded some inches in the treacherous sand. Then pressing all my weight on this foot I made a great effort, and tearing up the imbedded foot leaped to the firm sand, where I slipped and fell and for a few minutes panted with exhaustion.

I was saved, but Old Hoggen's head was gone forever.

Then I went toward the cliff, cautiously feeling my way, testing every spot on which my foot must rest, before trusting my weight to it. I gained the cliff, and resting on its firm base passed behind the fatal quicksand and went on my course to the stable strand beyond.

On I plodded till at last I came near a few houses built in a green cleft, whence through the cliffs a tiny stream, on whose banks stood the pretty village of Chidiock, fell into the sea.

There was a coast guard station here, with a little rope-railed plot, where before the row of trim houses the flagstaff rose.

As I drew near a coast guard and a policeman rushed toward me from behind a shed and grasped me on either side, holding me tight with a vigor which I felt to be quite disproportionate to the necessity of the occasion.

With the instinct of conscious innocence I struggled with them.

"Let me go!" I cried. "Let me go—what do you mean? Let me go I say!"

"Come now—none of this," said the policeman.

I still struggled.

"Better keep quiet," said the coast guard! "It's no use struggling."

"I will not keep quiet," I cried, struggling more frantically than ever.

The policeman looked at me right savagely and gave my neckcloth a twist which nearly strangled me. "Tell you what," he said sternly, "if you struggle any more, I'll whale you over the head with my baton."

I did not struggle anymore.

"Now," said he, "remember that I caution you that anything you say or do will be afterward used in evidence against you."

I thought a policy of conciliation was now best; so with what heartiness I could assume I said:

"My good fellow, you really make a mistake. Why you seize me I do not know."

"We know," he interrupted, with a hard laugh, "and if you say you don't know, why then you're a liar!"

I felt choking with anger. To be held is bad enough, but when the additional insult of calling one a liar is added, rage may surely be excused. My impulse on hearing the insult was to break free and strike the man, but he knew my intention and held me tighter.

"Take care!" he said, holding up his baton.

I took care.

"I ask you formally," I said with all my dignity, "on what authority do you treat me thus?"

"On this authority!" he answered, holding up his baton, and again laughing with his harsh, exasperating cachinnation. He playfully twirled his baton as if to impress upon me a sense of his proficiency in its use.

He then produced a pair of handcuffs, which were put on me. I struggled very hard, but the two men were too much for me, and I had to succumb.

He then began to search me. First he put his hand into the pocket of my shooting coat and pulled out the watch and chain. He looked at it with exultation.

"That is Old Hoggen's watch," I said.

"I know it is," he answered, at the same time pulling out the notebook and writing down my words. Next he produced the diamond ring, and the purse.

"That also," said I, "and that!"

Again he wrote down my words—this time in silence. Then he put in his hand again and drew it out, saying:

"Only wet paper!"

He next to put his hand into the other pocket, but drew it out again in an instant—not in silence this time.

"Curse the thing! What is it?"

I smiled as he lifted a crab out of the pocket with great carefulness. When he had got thus far, he continued:

"Now, young fellow, what have you got to say for yourself?"

For the last few minutes a very unpleasant thought had in my mind been growing to colossal proportions. It was evidence that I was being arrested for the murder of Old Hoggen, and here I was arrested when in possession of his property, but with no witnesses to prove my innocence, and with no trace of the lost man himself to substantiate my story. I began to be a little frightened as to the result.

"What I have to tell you is very strange," said I. "I left the Charmouth early this morning to walk to Bridport to get some crabs for my mother-in-law."

"Why, you have got crabs with you," said the policeman.

"I got them on the shore beyond," said I, pointing westward.

"Come! Stow that!" said the policeman. "That won't wash here. There isn't a crab to be found on the shore between Bridport and Lyme."

"That's true, anyhow. Every fool knows that!" added the coast guard.

I went on:

"I found the body of Old Hoggen floating in the water. I tried to carry it on here, but the storm came, and it was as much as I could do to escape. Besides, the body all feel in pieces, and at last—"

"A nice story that!" said the policeman. "But if it fell to bits, why didn't you bring one on with you?"

"I tried some, but they fell to bits."

"The head didn't," said he. "Why did you not bring it? Eh?"

"I did bring it," said I, "but I got into the quicksand and it was lost."

The coast guard struck in.

"There's only one bit of quicksand on all this coast, they say, for I never seen it myself. Why, man alive, it doesn't show once in twenty years."

"And the crabs?" asked the policeman.

"They were in Old Hoggen's body!"

"And what were you doing with them?"

"I was bringing them to my mother-in-law."

"Oh, the filthy scoundrel" ejaculated the coast guard.

"Did you carry them through the quicksand?" inquired the policeman.

"I did," said I, "and when I got out, I found that the big fellow had eaten the watch and was trying to swallow the ring."

The policeman and the coast guard seized me roughly, the latter saying:

"Come, take him off. He's the plumpest liar I ever seen."

"Let us finish the search first," said the policeman, as he renewed his investigations.

The thought that I was in a really suspicious position now began to make me most uncomfortable. "My poor wife! My poor wife!" I kept saying to myself.

The policeman, in his zeal, again put his hands in the pocket with the crabs, and drew it out with a yell. Then he took out the biggest crab, which by the way, as is sometimes the case, had one claw very much larger than the other. The left claw was the larger. He threw the crab on the shore and was about to stamp on it, when the coast guard put him back, saying:

"Avast, there, mate. Crabs isn't so plenty here that we walk on them. None here between Bridport and Lyme."

The policeman continued his search. He took the mass of wet papers and notes from the other pocket, and threw them on the ground, and went on diving into the recesses of the pockets. The coast guard was evidently struck with something, for he stooped and looked at the papers, turned them over, and fell down on his knees beside them with a loud cry. Then, in an excited whisper, he called out:

"Look here! Mate, look here! Its all money. It's thousands of pounds."

The constable also dropped beside the papers, and over the mass the two men gazed at each other with excited faces.

"Take care of it—take care!" said the policeman.

"You bet!" said the other shortly.

"What a fortune!"

The two men looked at each other, and then at me furtively, and somehow I felt that they have in common some vile instinct by which I was felt to be in the way. I remained, therefore, as passive as I could.

The two men eyed the papers. Said the coast guard:

"Where are the other things?"

"Here!" said the policeman, slapping his pocket.

"Better put them all together."

"Not at all. They are quite safe with me."

The two men looked at each other and seemed mutually to understand, for, without a word, the policeman took the watch and ring and purse from his pocket and laid them on the shore.

Both men eyed the lot greedily. Suddenly the policeman looked round and ran down the beach like a maniac, shouting, "Stop thief! Stop thief!" At the very edge of the water, he stopped and lifted the crab, which had been making its escape. He brought it back and laid on its back beside the other things. As he eyed the heap suspiciously, as if to see that nothing has been removed, he said, shaking his fist at the crab:

"You infernal brute, *you* may have been stealing something." The accent with which he said the word "you" was evidently meant as a caution and suspicion of the coast guard. The latter took it as such and said angrily:

"Stow that!"

The two men then proceeded to search me further. They took from me everything which could by any torturing of greed have been construed into a valuable. They opened a seem of my coat and turned out the lining.

Then, drawing away, they whispered a little together, and, returning to me, tied my legs together, put a gag in my mouth, and carried me round the point of a rock where we were out of sight of any chance comer. Then they brought hither the valuables, and, sitting down, began to record the worth of the lot.

One by one they open the bank notes and laid them flat. They were of all dates and numbers, and I felt as I looked that, from this fact, if once lost, there could be no possibility of tracing them. They laid the gold in a heap with the watch and the ring, and put the papers by themselves.

There was an immense amount of money—in gold only some 70 pounds, but in notes some 37,300 pounds.

When the two men had figured it all out, they looked at me with a look that made my blood run cold—for it meant murder.

Again they looked at each other, and, with a whisper, withdrew to a little distance.

I turned partly on my side so that I could watch them. There was no difficulty in this, and the fact of its being so added to my fear, for I knew that their being without fear of my taking notes of their movements meant that their minds were made up.

A short time sufficed them, and they turned again toward me. As they came, however, the bell of the old church at Chidiock began to ring. It was still early morning and the bell was for matins.

The coast guard stopped—some memory stirred within him, and with it came a doubt. He paused a moment and spoke:

"Mate."

The policeman realized the intention of mercy in the faltering tone, and answered as roughly and harshly as he could, turning quickly, almost threateningly, as he spoke.

"Well!"

"Mate, must we kill him? Wouldn't it do if he kept quiet, and let us get off with the money? No one knows the thing—why need they ever know?"

"He won't keep quiet," said the other. "Better cut his throat and bury him here in the sand."

The sailor looked at me, and, reading the inquiry in his eyes, I answered as well as I could with mine:

"I will be quiet!"

It was it plain as daylight that my life hung on the alternative, so I did not hesitate or falter.

I compounded a felony with a glance.

Notwithstanding my acquiescence, a violent discussion arose between the two men—the preserver of the peace being the more dangerous of the two.

The coast guard urged and argued that it were useless to commit a murder when the end they desired was insured. The policeman stuck persistently to his one point that were safer to cut my throat.

To me the anguish was intense. All the misdeeds of my life rose before me, and also every reason why life should be dear. I employed the sailor with my eyes to let me speak, and after a little while he removed the gag, after cautioning me that if I spoke above a whisper, my first syllable should be my last.

I whispered but one argument.

"If you kill me, I shall be sought after. You're safer as you are with my promise not to inform on you."

The argument was cogent, and told, and sound logic usually does. So, after a terrible threatening in case of my breaking my pledge, they untied my legs and took off the handcuffs.

Then they brought me into a boathouse by the beach in there brushed me and removed any traces of travel or violence. Next they put me into a pony cart that stood ready by the side of the laneway leading to Chidiock, and drove me into Charmouth, depositing me at my own door. We did not meet a single person by the way.

The last words I heard were the whisper caution of the policeman:

"No one has seen you or us. Go back to your bed and pretend you were never out," and then they drove off again.

I took the advice, slipped off my boots, and stole upstairs. My wife was still sleeping, so I undressed and got into bed. Lest I should wake her, I pretended to sleep, and soon despite my mental agitation, slept, too.

* * * *

I was awakened by my wife, who was up and dressed.

"Why, Augustus, you are desperately sleepy this morning. It is after 10 o'clock, and breakfast is over long ago. Cousin Jemima would not wait. However, your breakfast is kept hot."

I woke to broad consciousness, but thought it wise to feign heaviness.

"Never mind—I'll get up presently."

"But, my dear, you must get up now or you will miss the 'bus to Bridport. Remember, you promised to get some crabs for Cousin Jemima!"

"Oh, bother Cousin Jemima. There has been enough about crabs for one night." I said this with a sudden impulse and then stopped.

"Well, dear. I hope you have not had indigestion, too. Cousin Jemima says she has been very poorly and that it must have been from eating the new bread."

"Indeed!" said I, adding to myself, "I'm glad she suffered, too, for was all through her that I had that terrible ordeal to go through."

I got up and went downstairs. All was as usual; and presently I began to think I must have been dreaming. The idea grew; and the more I thought the matter over the more unreal and dreamlike it all seemed.

While, however, I was finishing my breakfast the servant came in and said there were two men at the door who had crabs to sell.

"Send them away at once," I called out, angrily. "I want no crabs."

The servant went, and return shortly, saying: "If you please, sir, they say that they hope you will buy a crab; they have one which was got between Bridport and Lyme."

This statement rather staggered me, for I felt a kind of dread that my late assailants had come to look me up. I told the servant I would see to the matter, and went out myself to the door. There stood two men—but not the least like the others. The coast guard was a small man with the big beard, and the policeman was a large man clean shaven. Of these two, one was large and the other small, but the large man had a bushy beard, and the small one was clean shaven. I thought that both men looked at me very hard, so I pretended not to notice anything except the subject of barter, and said as unconcernedly as I could:

"Well, my men, so I hear you have crabs to sell; let me look at them."

The big man answered: "We have only one left. Here it is!" and, looking at me very searchingly, he produced from a basket a crab with a big left claw and a small right one. I could not help a start of surprise which did not pass unnoticed, so I thought it better to be more unconcerned still, and said:

"No; that's not good enough. I think I do not care for it."

As I spoke, my wife approach the door, coming home, and with her my mother-in-law and Cousin Jemima.

The man did not notice them, but the big man said to me, civil enough"

"All right, sir. It does not matter, but I thought it well to show it to you."

As he was putting the crab back in the basket, Cousin Jemima saw it and came forward quickly.

"What is that, Augustus? Not a crab that you are sending away? You wretch!" the last words *sotto voce*.

After a little haggling she purchase the crab, which, strangely enough, the man seemed unwilling to sell her, and for which I had the additional pleasure of paying.

Cousin Jemima took the crab in triumph to the kitchen, and the men went away toward Axmouth.

When I went back to the sitting room, I was assailed on all sides. Cousin Jemima, in tears, said I had behaved like a brute—that I was sending away the only crab seen for days, just to vex and disappoint her.

My mother-in-law surmised that I did so because I wished to have to go over to Bridport, where, unnoticed I might play billiards and get tipsy, if not meet some "creature." Her daughter, to a small degree, shared her feelings—particularly the latter.

I maintained a strictly negative position.

* * * *

In the course of the day, the wife of the parson, George Edward Ancey, came to tea—her husband was a justice of the peace, and, as a perpetual resident, was practically the magistrate of the place. In the course of conversation she remarked that George Edward had been very much upset and worried in the morning. That two cases of insubordination had been before him. When was a coast guard, who had affronted his chief boatman before the other men, and who, on being severely censured, resigned on the spot, and had already left the village. The other was a policeman, who had refused to go on duty, and who had been accordingly summarily dismissed. Mr. Ancey regretted his departure, for he has been looked upon as the most trustworthy and active officer in the place.

When these small facts came to my knowledge, I felt more than ever in a perplexity, for their combination and the accurate manner in which they fitted into the history of the morning seemed conclusive proof that the whole thing was not a dream.

* * * *

Before supper time I went for a walk. As I was going out my wife said:

"Be sure to be home in time, Gus. There is a crab for supper and Cousin Jemima's going to dress herself—"

A walk on the beach did me good, for it cooled my brain, and in the serener atmosphere of the evening I began to believe again that the whole episode of finding Old Hoggen was a dream—a nightmare.

I returned home in a more cheerful humor, and, conscious of security and immunity from fear, felt kindly even to Cousin Jemima and tolerant of her foibles.

At the very threshold of my home my good resolution was tried.

On a chair in the hall sat Cousin Jemima awaiting my arrival, the very picture of grim, aggressive dissatisfaction. As I came in she sniffed—I saw that something was wrong and said nothing. She followed me into the dining room where, supper having just been served, my wife and her mother were seated.

"I said we would not wait a single moment for you, after conduct," the latter..

"What's up now?" said I.

"What's up indeed!"—this with indignant sarcasm. "A nice gentlemanly trick to play upon two ladies whose appetite are not good."

"O-h-h," I said, with what I certainly intended to be utmost sarcasm spoken in the most polished way, "then you allude to something I've done by letter."

"By letter? Certainly not! What are you talking about?"

"You said I played a trick on two ladies whose appetites were not good, and I presume I must have done so by letter. Do not see? The someone must be at the long distance from this, for I know no one here answering the description."

"You brute!" was the comment of Cousin Jemima, while my mother-in-law said nothing, but glared at her daughter, who smiled.

I sat down and tried to make matters a little pleasanter.

"Come now mother," I said "tell me what I've done and what it is all about."

"The crab," said Cousin Jemima, in tones at once sepulchral and hysterical.

"Well, what about it?"

"You did it on purpose."

"What did I do? I am all in surprise."

Here my wife struck in.

"The fact is, dear, that the crab was a fraud, and mamma and Cousin Jemima, seeing that you were talking to the men, imagine that you got the whole thing up for a joke—that it was, in fact, what you call a 'plant'."

"My dear, I am no nearer to the fact than I was. How was the crab a fraud?"

"Well, you see there was something very queer about it. It was quite fresh, you know, and all that, but it had been opened and was all cut to little bits with knives and then put back again, just as if someone has been searching it."

Here was a staggering proof that I had not dreamed. I almost gasped for breath and felt that I turned white.

The three women notice the change.

"Are you ill, dear?" said my wife.

"He might well be," said her mother.

"Served him right!" said Cousin Jemima.

I recovered myself in a moment, and laughed as well as I could.

"You are a parcel of sillies, and I know nothing about it. Why, it was you, Cousin Jemima, who bought the crab."

After a while the conversation changed to other topics. I was now beset by a most extraordinary doubt. Was my whole adventure a dream, or was it not?

I can not tell.

* * * *

Some three months after our return to town, we read in the *South Dorset News*, which some of our seaside friends sent us regularly, the following paragraph:

THE MYSTERY OF MR HOGGEN

"The strange mystery regarding the late Mr. Jabez Hoggen—the Charmouth millionaire—whose disappearance set Dorset and neighboring counties in a blaze, has at last been cleared up. Our readers will of course remember the disappearance early in August last of Mr. Hoggen, whose wealth and eccentricity were fruitful topics of conversation not only in the quiet village of Charmouth, his native place—but through all the neighboring country. Lyme, on the one hand, and Bridport on the other, and the inland towns of Axminster and Chard, were well acquainted with the name of the wealthy eccentric. Mr. Hoggen was very retired and uncommunicative, and it so came to pass that when his disappearance became known not a single person could even guess at any motive or cause for such a fact. No one was in his confidence. It was for a time generally supposed that he had been murdered for the sake of his reputed wealth, and suspicion was by the police baselessly attached to certain of the summer visitors of our pleasant Dorset coast. Our contemporary, the *Bridport Banner*, with that gross bad taste which, equally with its mendacity, characterizes its utterances, suggested—if we remember aright, the ribald shrieking forced upon our ears by some drunken Conservative reeking with the scurrilous falsity of some paltry true blue (?) meeting—for we do not read the rag—that perhaps Mr. Hoggen had in his old age seen the error of his ways, and, overcome with remorse for his adherence to the principles of liberalism, committed suicide. Time had given the lie, as it ever does, to such paltry attacks upon the noble dead. It has come to light that Mr. Hoggen took a passage in the name of Smith for Queensland in the *Tamar Indien*, sailing from Southampton on the 26th of August. We are justified in supposing that the poor gentleman, oppressed with the decadent spirit which allow such vile rags as the Conservative organs to flourish in this once pure soil, and longing for the purer atmosphere where the pollution of atmosphere caused by Conservatism is not, left in sorrow his native shore. He was recognized on board by a native of Charmouth—one Miles Ruddy, a steward on the *Tamar Indien*. It appears that he was much upset by the recognition. The following evening, as the bell was sounding for the putting out of the ship's lights, a splash was heard, and the dread cry

'Man Overboard' was raised. Every effort was made to save the life of the human creature, whose head was seen for a few minutes bobbing up and down among the foam that marked the mighty vessel's track. But without avail. He never rose, and the ship was compelled to proceed on her course. A muster of the crew and passengers showed that the missing man was Jabez Smith, or, more properly, Jabez Hoggen. The dispositions of the captain and officers of the ship and of several of the chief passengers regarding the events have been registered in Queensland, and we hasten to lay the facts just arrived by the mail before our readers."

A little time passed, and in some two months there appeared in the same print the following paragraph:

STRANGE HISTORY OF TWO CHARMOUTH MEN.

"The Australian mail just in bring from Victoria the details, as far as they are known, of a romance, unhappily tragic, concerning two late inhabitants of Charmouth. It appears that the two men, but a few months ago well known in our pleasant Dorset village, one having been a policeman and the other a coast guard, had but lately arrived in Melbourne. At first they did not seem of much account, but before long met with a lucky stroke of fortune—alas!—fatal to them. After but a short absence, presumably in the northern gold fields, they had evidently made some wonderfully lucky discoveries of gold pockets, for on their return they made such purchases of land and houses as showed that they must have been at the time possessed of great wealth. Suddenly they had quarreled, for some unknown reason, sold again their property, and together disappeared up country. A few days later the bodies, greatly mutilated, were discovered among the charred ruins of a deserted camp. They had either fought and killed each other, or they had been murdered. The fire of the camp had spread and partially consumed the bodies, so that nothing definite could be ascertained. In this romantic story we may read as we run of the vanity of wealth."

When I read the paragraph, I felt my mind relieved, for here was assurance to me that I had not dreamed.

* * * *

One evening long afterward I told my wife and her mother and Cousin Jemima the whole story.

My wife came and put her arms around me and whispered:

"Augustus, dear—you may have dreamed—I hope so; but, thank God, you are spared to us!"

My mother-in-law said:

"I think you might have managed to keep some of the money, but you never do as you ought in such things. At any rate, you might have told us before this, but I suppose you have so much to conceal that things like this get lost among them."

Cousin Jemima, after frowning a while and pursing her lips as if thinking, said, sniffing:

"I believe it's all a lie!"

"My dear Cousin Jemima!" I remonstrated.

"Well! Suppose it's not," she answered, sharply, "at any rate, you took the crabs from Old Hoggen's body and brought them here—no you didn't bring them here, but you let me buy them—to eat! Ugh!! You brute!!!"

I am still in doubt about the whole affair.

Was it a dream?

I do not know!